Sleepover Fun

Story by Pamela Rushby
Illustrations by Nikolett Timar

Contents

Chapter 1

A Busy, Noisy House

Mason lived with his mum and dad
and his brothers and sisters,
in a house that was always busy and full of noise.
They had a dog and three scrambling puppies.

Mum liked to mow the lawn.
She had a very noisy lawnmower.

Dad was learning to play the trumpet.
When he played his trumpet, Dad made even more noise
than Mum's lawnmower.

Sometimes, Mason wished his family was a bit quieter.

2

Mason had been invited to Samar's house for a sleepover. Samar was a new boy at school. Mason liked him.

I hope we will be friends for a long time, thought Mason as he packed an overnight bag.

Chapter 2

A Very Quiet House

On Saturday, Mason arrived at Samar's place.
He found that things at Samar's place
were very different from those at his house.

There was just Samar and his mum in Samar's family.
They lived in a high-rise apartment.

"Try to keep quiet, boys," said Samar's mum.
"We mustn't bother the neighbours."

Samar had a room all to himself.
He had plenty of books, games and toys.

"Wow!" said Mason. "You have a laptop!
And you have your own TV!
And a game console! Can we play a video game?"

"Sure," said Samar.

Later, they watched a movie on Samar's TV.

At bedtime, Samar pulled out an extra bed from underneath his bed.
Keeping their voices down, the boys talked and laughed until it was very late.

When Mason arrived home the next day, his sisters were riding their scooters up and down the path.
His dad was playing the trumpet.

Inside, Mason's brothers were kicking a ball up and down the hallway. Mason took his bag to his room and closed the door behind him. He wished his house was more like Samar's quiet apartment.

Chapter 3

Samar Comes for a Sleepover

The next week, Mum said to Mason, "Would you like to invite Samar for a sleepover this weekend?"

"Oh," said Mason. "I don't know."

“Didn’t you enjoy yourself at Samar’s place?” asked Mum.

“I had a great time,” Mason replied.

“You should ask him, then!” said Mum.

Mason frowned. He didn’t have a game console
or his own TV – or even his own room.
Would Samar be bored if he came over?
What would they do?

Samar said to Mason that he would love to come for a sleepover that weekend.

All week, Mason worried about Samar coming over.

On Saturday, Mason's dad brought a blow-up mattress into the boys' room.
"Where can we put it?" asked Mason.

"If you pick up some of those clothes and toys, there'll be room," said Dad.

When Samar arrived, Mason wondered what they could do. They sat on Mason's bunk.

Just then, Mason's sister Lulu walked past the door. "We're all building a fort from cardboard boxes in the backyard," she said. "Come and help us!"

Mason thought about Samar's video games and laptop. "Samar wouldn't want to build a fort," he said to Lulu.

"Yes, I would!" said Samar. "That would be fun!"

So Mason and Samar helped the others to build the fort.

"Now we're going to make a ramp to ride our scooters over!" said Mason's brother Ethan.

"Samar wouldn't want to do that," said Mason.

"Yes, I would!" said Samar. "That sounds like great fun!"

Chapter 4

Two Different Sleepovers

That evening, Mason's family had a barbecue in the backyard.

"I think I'll get my trumpet," said Mason's dad, after dinner.

"Oh nooo, Dad!" shouted everyone. "You're terrible!"
Dad got his trumpet anyway.
It sounded better when they all sang along as Dad played.

When they went to bed, Mason said to Samar,
"I didn't think you'd like it at my place.
My family can be so noisy."

"I didn't think you'd like it at *my* place," said Samar.
"It's just Mum and me, so it can be really quiet."

The boys laughed.

"Maybe I can come to your place when I want to play video games and watch movies in bed," said Mason.

"And I'll come to yours when I want to build things, and sing really loudly," said Samar.

"And we'll both have fun!" said Mason.